HILDA HEN'S SCARY NIGHT

For Lucy and her cousins

MARY WORMELL

HILDA HEN'S SCARY NIGHT

HARCOURT BRACE & COMPANY
San Diego New York London
Printed in Hong Kong

One sunny afternoon Hilda Hen fell asleep underneath a rosebush.

When she woke up it was nighttime.
“Oh dear,” clucked Hilda.
“It’s so dark. I must get back to the henhouse.”
It looked very far away.
Hilda set off nervously.

“Oh my goodness, there’s a snake!” gasped Hilda.
“What shall I do?”
She thought for a moment.
“I’ll just have to tiptoe past as quietly as I can.”

Hilda tiptoed carefully past the snake.
"I didn't know I could be so brave,"
she clucked proudly.

But just then . . .

“Oh help, a monster!” squawked Hilda.
“What shall I do?”
She thought for a moment.
“I’ll just have to fly past as high as I can.”

Hilda flapped frantically and flew
past the monster.
“I didn’t know I could fly so high,”
she clucked proudly.

But just then . . .

"Oh my word, a lake!" shrieked Hilda.
"What shall I do?"
She thought for a moment.
"I'll just have to swim as best I can."

Hilda splashed awkwardly across
the lake.
"I didn't know I could swim so well,"
she clucked proudly.

But just then . . .

“Oh no, a fox,” whispered Hilda.
“What shall I do?”
She thought for a moment.
“I’ll just have to run as fast as I can.”

Hilda scuttled past the fox.
"I didn't know I could run so fast,"
she clucked proudly.

But just then . . .

"Oh dear, I'm under a strange bridge.
I must be lost!" cried Hilda.
"What shall I do?"
But before she could think, the bridge moved.

Hilda got such a fright that she jumped high
into the air.
“Oh, I can see the henhouse from here. It’s a good
thing I can jump so high,” she clucked proudly.

She hurried on to the henhouse and arrived just
as everyone was getting up for breakfast.
"Oh, I'm so glad I'm back," clucked Hilda.
"I've had such a scary night."

"There are so many scary things in the farmyard at night," sighed Hilda.
"I wonder where they all go during the day?"
The other hens looked across the yard, and they all wondered, too.

First published in Great Britain 1996 by
Victor Gollancz

First U.S. edition 1996

Library of Congress Cataloging-in-Publication Data
Wormell, Mary.
Hilda Hen's scary night/Mary Wormell.
p. cm.
Summary: During her nighttime journey to the henhouse Hilda Hen finds unexpected courage within herself as she tiptoes past a snake, runs from a fox, and swims a lake.
ISBN 0-15-200990-6
[1. Chickens—Fiction. 2. Night—Fiction.
3. Courage—Fiction.]
I. Title.
PZ7.W88774Hh 1996
[E]—dc20 95-15525

The text and display type was set in Bramley Medium.

H G F E D C B